DYLAN'S DRAGON

Annie Silvestro

illustrated by Ben Whitehouse

Albert Whitman & Company
Chicago, Illinois

Dylan spent his days playing.
Doodling, drawing, daydreaming.

But as Dylan grew, there was so much more to do...

and do...

and do.

Every second was planned, every moment
measured, every day completely, utterly full.

So when Dragon first showed up, it was, of course, at a very inconvenient time.

"Hi!" said Dylan.

Dragon smiled expectantly.

"Sorry," said Dylan. "I have school. Can you play later?"

Dragon huffed, which felt hot like a suntan but sounded like *yes*.

All day long Dylan wondered about Dragon.
He seemed oddly familiar.

After school, Dylan raced off the bus.
Dragon was waiting for him.
Dylan flung his backpack and climbed onto Dragon's back.
They soared in circles through the air...

Until Dylan's mom called, "Let's go! Time for piano!"
Dragon dipped down and dropped Dylan at the door.
"Thanks," said Dylan.

The next morning, Dragon gave him a ride to breakfast.
Too soon, Dylan heard the bus pull up.

"See you after school?"
Dragon stuck out his tongue and slurped oatmeal off
Dylan's cheek, which felt kind of slimy but seemed like a yes.

After school, Dylan and Dragon took flight.
Until...
"Homework time," called his dad.
"Ten more minutes?" begged Dylan.

After what felt like ten seconds, Dylan's
mom called from the kitchen window.
"Dylan! You have to study for your math
test before you go to science club!"

Dylan drooped.
"Maybe you can help me?"
Dylan and Dragon raced inside.
But Dragon nearly set his math review on fire.
Dragon quickly stamped out the smoke with his foot.

"Phew," said Dylan.

On Wednesday came baseball practice.
Dragon suited up.
But Dylan's coach had a strict no-dragon policy.

On Thursday, Dylan had a dentist appointment.
"Come with me," he said. "You'll get a prize at the end!"
Dragon flashed his perfect teeth and shook his head.

On Friday came karate class.
Dragon showed Dylan his moves.
Dylan thought he'd better stay behind.

"Can you play tomorrow?" asked Dylan. "It's the weekend."
Dragon snorted.
Then he swatted Dylan with his tail, which felt cold and scaly
but had to mean yes.

On Saturday, Dylan threw off his covers.

"Let's play!" he told Dragon.

As he and Dragon headed for the door, his mom reminded him he had a baseball game.

And a piano recital.

And his Aunt Edith's ninetieth birthday party.

"But...but..." stammered Dylan.

He looked at his father.
He looked at his mother.
"When do I get to play?"
"Sorry, bud. Not today," said his dad.
"Go get ready."

On Sunday morning, Dylan slept in.
His mom peeked in to check on him.
"What do we have to do now?" he asked, yawning.
"Absolutely nothing," said his mom. "Just go out and play."
"Play?
"Hooray!
"Did you hear that, Dragon?"

But Dragon wasn't there.
Dylan couldn't find him anywhere.
It seemed like Dragon was draGONE.

Dylan checked under his bed.

In his closet.

In the playroom.
"Dragon!" he called. "I can play now! Really!"

He checked in the garage.

In the backyard.

On the front steps.
"Come back!"

Dylan wiped away tears.

"What's wrong?" asked his mom.

"I can't find Dragon anywhere!"

"Dragon?"

"He's my friend," sniffed Dylan. "And I never have time to play with him. We always have so much to do."

"Sounds like we need to cut back."

Dylan nodded.
"How about I help you find Dragon.
What does he look like?"
"I'll show you."
Dylan raced to get his crayons.

And just like that, he remembered.

Back when he had time to doodle and daydream, Dylan had drawn that Dragon!

And he could do it again.

Colors blazed from his crayons as he drew every dazzling detail.

When he finished, Dylan carried the picture downstairs.
As he walked, the drawing grew warm.
Then hot.
Then hotter.
The paper shook...

It smoked...
then POOF popped Dragon, right into the living room.

"You're back!" cried Dylan.
But really, he had never left.
"Want to play?"
The dragon unfurled his wings and wrapped them
around Dylan, which felt like a warm hug...

and was most definitely a yes!

For Sam and Charlie, better than I could have ever imagined.
I love you.—AS

For Yvonne, Timmy, Mathias, Mam, Pap, and Tom.
Thank you for everything.—BW

Library of Congress Cataloging-in-Publication data
is on file with the publisher.
Text copyright © 2021 by Annie Silvestro
Illustrations copyright © 2021 by Albert Whitman & Company
Illustrations by Ben Whitehouse
First published in the United States of America
in 2021 by Albert Whitman & Company
ISBN 978-0-8075-1742-0 (hardcover)
ISBN 978-0-8075-1743-7 (ebook)

Printed in China
10 9 8 7 6 5 4 3 2 1 WKT 24 23 22 21 20

Design by Valerie Hernández

For more information about Albert Whitman & Company,
visit our website at www.albertwhitman.com.